First published in the United States of America in 2016
by Chronicle Books LLC. Simultaneously published in Italy
in 2016 by Maurizio Corraini srl.

Library of Congress Cataloging-in-Publication Data
Names: Ahn, Somin, author, illustrator.
Title: One minute / Somin Ahn.
Description: San Francisco, California : Chronicle Books LLC, [2016] |
Summary: In simple text and illustrations, the author explains all the things
that can happen in a minute—both good and bad.
Identifiers: LCCN 2016005733 | ISBN 9781452155647 (alk. paper)
Subjects: LCSH: Time—Juvenile fiction. | Time perception—Juvenile fiction.
| CYAC: Time—Fiction.
Classification: LCC PZ7.1.A35 On 2016 | DDC [E]--dc23 LC
record available at http://lccn.loc.gov/2016005733

Manufactured in China.

Design by CorrainiStudio.
Hand lettering by Somin Ahn.

10 9 8 7 6 5 4 3 2 1

Chronicle Books LLC
680 Second Street
San Francisco, California 94107

Chronicle Books—we see things differently.
Become part of our community at www.chroniclekids.com.

SOMIN AHN
ONE MINUTE

chronicle books · san francisco

One minute is sixty seconds.
In one minute, the second hand
moves sixty times while the long
hand moves once.

In one minute, you
blink your eyes 20 times,

and your hair grows
.00068 centimeters.

In one minute, you
can hug your dog...

say hi to your neighbor...

or plant seeds.

Sometimes one minute is short.

Sometimes one minute is long.

But if you are with your
best friends, it is short again.

Sometimes one minute is important.

SUPERMARK

Sometimes one minute is nothing.

In one minute,
something can happen.

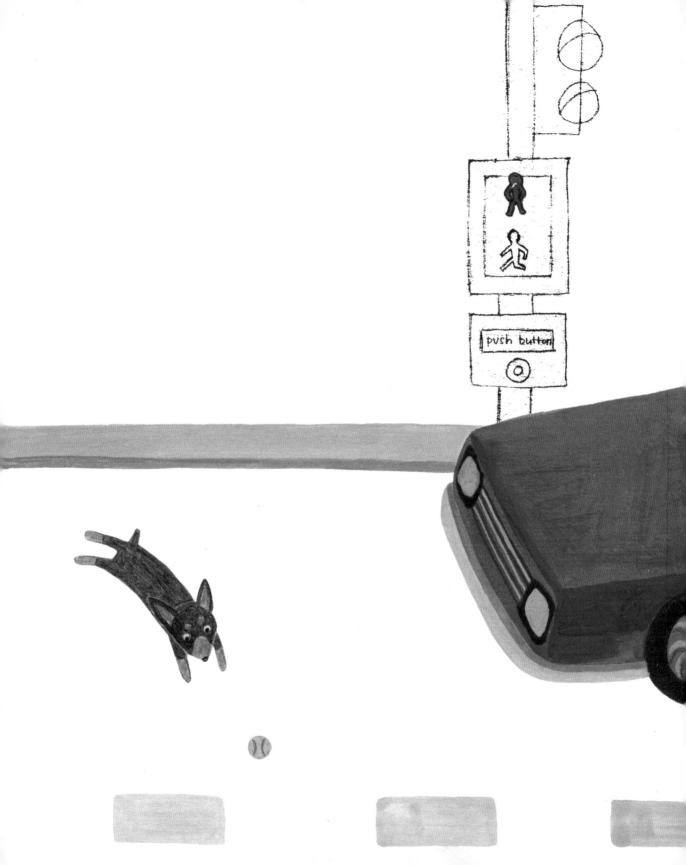

Or something can be saved.

In one minute, someone can leave.

And someone can arrive.